THE
FAMOUS FIVE

ANNUAL 2014

BOOKS IN THE FAMOUS FIVE SERIES

The Famous Five Short Story Collection

All available from Hodder Children's books

THE
FAMOUS
FIVE
ANNUAL 2014

Hodder
Children's
Books

A division of Hachette Children's Books

With special thanks to Tony Summerfield, for his advice and assistance with source material, and to Norman Wright, for permission to use material from *The Famous Five: Everything You Ever Needed to Know*.

For more information about the Famous Five, visit the website of the Enid Blyton Society at www.enidblytonsociety.co.uk

First published in Great Britain in 2013 by Hodder Children's Books

The right of Enid Blyton to be identified as the Author of the Work has been asserted by her in accordance with the Copyright, Designs and Patents Act 1988

1

A Catalogue record for this book is available from the British Library

ISBN 978 1 444 91442 9

Printed and bound in China by WKT

The paper and board used in this hardback by Hodder Children's Books are natural recyclable products made from wood grown in sustainable forests. The manufacturing processes conform to the environmental regulations of the country of origin.

Hodder Children's Books
a division of Hachette Children's Books
338 Euston Road, London NW1 3BH
An Hachette UK company

www.hachette.co.uk
famousfivebooks.com

CONTENTS

TIMMY'S TIMELINE

Here's how it all began – and how the Famous Five phenomenon has spread throughout the world.

1942 The first Famous Five novel was published – *Five On a Treasure Island*. For many years, the books were available only in hardback editions, which are now highly collectible.

1947 The first Famous Five book to be serialised, *Five Go off to Camp*, was in *Sunny Stories*. It was the only Famous Five book in this publication.

1950 The first Famous Five Book – *Five on a Treasure Island*, was published in America.

1951 The Famous Five card game was launched by Pepys. It was later redesigned so the characters' likenesses matched the TV actors'!

1952 The hugely successful Famous Five club was launched, as part of Enid Blyton's charitable works to help children recovering from illness.

Tens of thousands of children joined and their fundraising helped establish a Famous Five ward at Great Ormond Street Hospital in London.

1953 *Five Go Down to the Sea* was the first Famous Five novel to be serialised in *Enid Blyton's Magazine*. A further three novels were all serialised in this publication.

The first Famous Five book, *Fünf Freunde erforschen die Schatzinsel* (*Five on a Treasure Island*), was published in Germany by Büchert Verlag.

1954 The first Famous Five short story, 'A Lazy Afternoon', was published in *Enid Blyton's Magazine Annual No. 1*. A further seven short stories followed in various publications.

1955 Enid Blyton wrote a stage play about the Famous Five, which was performed at Princes Theatre in London – she helped cast the children in the starring roles, and attended several of the rehearsals.

The first Famous Five jigsaw puzzle, *Five in Camp,* was released. Twenty were created in total, all illustrated by Eileen Soper (who is famous, of course, for illustrating the books).

The first Famous Five French edition, *Le Club des Cinq* (*Five Go Adventuring Again*), was published and the first Dutch edition, *De Vijf en het gestrande goudschip* (*Five on a Treasure Island*), was published.

1957 *Five On a Treasure Island* was produced as eight sixteen-minute films by the Children's Film Foundation.

1960 The first Famous Five Portuguese edition, *Os Cinco na Ilha do Tesouro* (*Five on a Treasure Island*), was published.

1963 Enid Blyton published the last of the Famous Five novels – *Five Are Together Again* – which was the 21st in the series.

1964 The Children's Film Foundation released *Five Have a Mystery to Solve* as six films.

The first Famous Five Spanish edition, *Los Cinco y el tesoro de la isla* (*Five on a Treasure Island*), was published.

1967 The Famous Five were published in mass market paperback editions for the first time by Knight.

1975 Whitman released the first of eight jigsaws, *Five on a Treasure Island*.

Philips released the first Famous Five LP record, *Five on a Treasure Island*. They also released *Five Have a Mystery to Solve*.

1977 The first *Famous Five Annual* was published, based on *Famous Five on a Hike Together*, told in a mix of illustrated text and a comic strip. A further eight annuals followed and there was then an eleven year gap before another annual was published in 1996, based on the new television series.

1978-9 Southern Television broadcast hugely popular dramatisations of all the books – apart from *Five On a Treasure Island*, *Five Have a Mystery To Solve* and *Five Have Plenty of Fun*.

Whitman produced a Famous Five board game, *Famous Five Kirrin Island Treasure Quest*. Apart from the two card games, this is the only Famous Five game that was ever marketed.

1981 Anthea Bell's translation of French author Claude Voilier's Famous Five continuation novels began being translated into English. Other 'spin-offs' have been published since, including *The Famous Five Adventure Game Books* (1984), *The Famous Five and You* (1987-89) and *Just George* (2000).

1982 A comedy spoof of the Famous Five, *Five Go Mad in Dorset*, was aired on Channel 4's first night of broadcasting. It's famous for featuring Dawn French and Jennifer Saunders and for the phrase 'lashings of ginger beer'. It's fun – but has nothing to do with the novels written by Enid Blyton. They produced a second film the following year, *Five Go Mad on Mescalin*.

1983 Rainbow released the first dramatised cassette of the Famous Five, *Five Run Away Together*. They also released *Five Go to Smuggler's Top*.

1985 *Enid Blyton's Adventure Magazine* was published, featuring full-colour strip cartoons based on the stories. As with the Television series the first was titled *Five on Kirrin Island* (dropping the word 'Again' from the sixth book) and it was followed by 16 further titles. The four titles that were not used were *Five Fall into Adventure*, *Five Have a Wonderful Time*, *Five on a Secret Trail* and *Five Are Together Again*.

1995–7 A brand new TV series saw all the novels adapted by Zenith North.

Five Have a Puzzling Time, published by Red Fox, brought together eight Famous Five short stories which Enid wrote for various publications and promotions.

1996 The Famous Five Musical (based on *Five Go Adventuring* Again) toured around Britain, visiting places such as Bath, Canterbury and Woking.

The first Famous Five CD-ROM, *Five on a Treasure Island*, was released by S.I.R.

1997 To mark Enid Blyton's Centenary, the Royal Mail issued a set of stamps, one of which featured the Famous Five.

2008 Disney launched a TV cartoon series featuring the children of the Famous Five. Sometimes, the original characters and stories are referenced, but they bear little resemblance to Enid Blyton's originals.

2012 Hodder Children's Books celebrated the Five's 70th anniversary with special editions featuring covers by Quentin Blake, Helen Oxenbury, Emma Chichester Clark, Chris Riddell and Oliver Jeffers – in association with the charity House of Illustration.

MEET JULIAN

Julian is a tall, sturdy, good-looking boy with a determined face and brown eyes. He is the oldest of the Five (twelve years old when we first meet him) and as their adventures progress he considers himself to be leader of the group, particularly when they are away from home on one of their many holidays. In fact, when they are going off on a cycling tour in *Five Get Into Trouble*, Uncle Quentin pays him the compliment of saying

'I'd bank on Julian to keep the others in order and see they were all safe and sound.'

He has good leadership skills, gets on well with people and has a wide general knowledge. Julian is good at finding his way around, having what is described in the books as a 'jolly good bump of locality' – which is Enid Blyton's way of saying that he can read a map and use a compass well!

At times Julian tries to be too over-protective and when, in *Five Go Off in a Caravan*, he suggests that he should lock

Anne and George in their caravan at night for their safety George won't have it, replying that Timmy is far better protection than any lock.

In the early adventures George often appears to be leader of the Five but as they grow older Julian usually takes command – although George won't always accept his leadership without a challenge and on some occasions, as in *Five Are Together Again*, she totally ignores his 'orders'. When Dick finds Julian a bit too bossy he usually carries out orders but will jokingly call Julian 'Captain', or tell him that he reminds him of their headmaster!

Some of the villains met by the Five in their adventures find that Julian has a very good way with words and a ready tongue when it comes to answering back. The unpleasant Mr Stick, who is staying with his equally unpleasant wife at Kirrin Cottage while Uncle Quentin and Aunt Fanny are away, thinks that he can keep the Five half starved and under his thumb, but in a battle of words with Julian over the contents of the larder Mr Stick comes out a poor loser. Hunchy, at Owl's Dene, also finds himself at a loss for words when he argues with Julian.

Julian gets on well with responsible adults, as he has 'a polite, well mannered way with him that all the grown ups liked.' He is helpful and caring to those in need but keen to help the police track down the robbers, kidnappers, crooks and other villains that the Five regularly encounter in their adventures.

GEORGE'S HAIR IS TOO LONG

'It's so hot on Kirrin Beach,' said Julian. 'Windy Cove will be nice and cool. There's always a breeze blowing there.'

'Well, I wanted to go and have my hair cut,' said George. 'Honestly, it will be as long as Anne's if I don't have it cut soon.'

'We pass the hairdresser's on the way to Windy Cove,' said Julian. 'We'll all go into the ice-cream shop and have ices, and wait for you there.'

'The shop's shut! It's early-closing day,' George shouted. 'I forgot. Now I can't have my hair cut.'

'I shall go and borrow some scissors in the ironmonger's,' shouted George. 'Mr. Pails will let me in at the side-door. You go on with Timmy and have ice-creams. I'll catch you up when I'm ready.'

George went down the passage that led to the shop and the old fellow took her to a drawer at the back. At that very moment the door was forced open and two men came hurriedly into the shop.

At first they didn't see Mr. Pails and George, and made for the little black safe set at the back of the counter. Mr. Pails gave an indignant shout. 'Hey, you! What do you mean, forcing your way in here? I'll ...'

But one of the men leapt over to him and put his hand over the old fellow's mouth. The other man ran to George and swung her into a little cupboard nearby, paying no attention to her yells. Mr. Pails was shoved in, too, and the door was forced shut on them and locked.

George shouted at the top of her voice, and so did Mr. Pails. But the shop was set apart from the others in the street, and there was no one to hear them on that hot, stifling afternoon.

George heard the sound of panting as the men removed the heavy little safe. Then the shop-door shut, and there was the sound of a van being started up — and driven away!

The others had now finished their ice-creams and were on the way to Windy Cove, Timmy lagging behind a little on the look-out for his beloved George. Why didn't she come? He suddenly decided to go back and look for her. He felt anxious, though he didn't know why. He turned tail and trotted off back to the village.

Suddenly a van turned a corner behind them and came racing up at top speed. Dick only just dragged Anne out of its way in time. The van swerved and went on, hooting wildly at the next corner.

'What does the driver think he's doing?' said Dick angrily. 'Tearing down narrow, winding lanes like that! What's his hurry?'

The van turned the corner – and almost immediately after, there came an explosive noise and the scream of brakes. Then a silence.

'Whew! That sounded like a burst tyre,' said Julian, beginning to run. 'I hope they haven't had an accident.'

The three turned the corner. They saw the van slewed round in the lane, almost in the ditch. The tyre on the left-hand back wheel was flat and had split badly. It was a very burst tyre indeed! Two men were looking at it angrily.

'Here, you!' said one of the men, turning to Dick. 'Run to the nearest garage, will you, and ask a man to come and help us?'

'Certainly not!' said Dick. 'You nearly knocked over my sister just now. One of you can go and get help yourselves. You'd no business to drive along a country lane like that.'

But neither of the men made a move to go back for help. Instead, they scowled at the burst tyre and at each other. The three stood there, looking with interest at the angry men.

'You clear off,' said one of the men at last. 'Unless you want to help us with the wheel. Do you know how to change a wheel?'

'Yes,' said Julian, sitting down on the hedge bank. 'Don't you? It's funny if you don't know. As your job is driving a van, I should have thought it would be one of the first things you'd learn!'

'You shut up,' said the first man, 'and clear off.'

Anne didn't like all this. 'I think I'll go back and meet George,' she said, and walked round the van. She took a quick look inside – and saw a little black safe there! A safe! She took a quick glance back at the two men. They certainly were a nasty-looking couple. She went over to Julian and sat down beside him. She took a twig and began to write idly in the thick dust at their feet, nudging him as she did so.

'A safe is in the van.' Anne knew that the boys had seen what she had written, she rubbed her foot over the hurried writing.

The three stared at the two men, who were now trying to change the wheel. It was plain that they had never changed one before! Julian caught hold of Anne when she got up to go back and meet George.

Poor George had stood in the cupboard till she was so cramped that she could hardly move an arm or leg. Mr. Pails seemed to have fainted, but she couldn't do anything about it. And then she heard a most familiar and welcome sound!

Feet pattered down the passage that led to the back of the shop, and then came a whine. Timmy!

'Timmy! Tim, I'm here, in this cupboard!' called George. 'Timmy!'

Timmy came and scraped at the cupboard, and then began to bark so furiously that a passer-by stopped in surprise. He pushed at the door, which had been left unlocked by the two thieves, and looked inside. He saw Timmy at once. The dog ran to him and then back to the cupboard, still barking.

'I'll send someone for the police – and a doctor, too,' said the man. 'You sit down in that chair, Mr. Pails. I'll look after you.'

And then, round the corner came George at last, with Timmy at her heels. Rather a pale George, evidently bursting with news. She raced up to them.

'Ju! Dick! What do you think happened to me? Mr. Pails and I were locked in a cupboard in his shop by two thieves who …'

She suddenly caught sight of the two men tinkering with the van, and stopped, astounded. She pointed at them and shouted.

'Why – those are the two men! And that's the van they came in – have they got a safe in it?'

A big car came round the corner. Julian waved to it to stop. Two men were in it.
'What's up?' they called. Julian explained as shortly as he could.

One of the men jumped down immediately. 'Let's put that wheel on, and take the two men back to Kirrin Village. I can drive it, and the boy with the dog can come, too – we'll put him in the van with the two men! You others can get into my car, and we'll follow the van back to Kirrin and get the police!'

Timmy, and George (pleased because she had been mistaken for a boy!) sat in the front of the van with the man from the other car. They drove off, followed by the big car, in which sat a pleased and smiling Julian, Dick and Anne!

It was very exciting when they all got to Kirrin Village! The police were amazed and delighted to have the two robbers safely delivered to them, with the safe *and* the stolen van!
'Well – what a thrill!' said George's mother, when they arrived home at last and told their astonishing tale. 'So you didn't get to Windy Cove, after all. Still – you can all go tomorrow!'

'I can't,' said George at once.
'WHY?' asked everyone, surprised.
'Because – I simply – *must* – get – my – hair – cut!' said George. 'And I'll jolly well see I'm not locked in a cupboard *next* time!'

MEET GEORGE

George has many excellent qualities. She has a kind heart, is loyal to her friends and is absolutely truthful.

Georgina wishes that she were a boy and insists on wearing boys' clothes and having her hair cut very short. She will only answer to the name of George and ignores anyone who calls her Georgina. When Julian, Dick and Anne first meet their cousin they find her a fierce, hot-tempered, lonely little girl with

blue eyes, short curly hair, a rather sulky mouth and a fierce frown. She enjoys her own company and believes that as long as she has her beloved dog, Timmy, she does not need friends. As she gets to know her three cousins she begins to change, gradually realising that things are much more fun if she shares them.

By the end of their first adventure she is a much friendlier person and her happiness is made complete when she is allowed to have Timmy back at Kirrin Cottage. She had never been to school when her cousins first meet her but after *Five On A Treasure Island* she goes to Gaylands School with Anne.

She excels at many outdoor activities and is a wonderful swimmer, rope thrower and climber. She drives the pony and trap kept by the family and can row splendidly, particularly when negotiating the dangerous rocks around Kirrin Island. She has 'the sharpest ears of the lot' and we are told 'no one had such good eyes as George.'

Although she changes for the better after their first adventure George never loses her hot temper or her frown and displays both when she is annoyed or not allowed to have her own way; but as Dick comments in *Five Go Off in a Caravan*, 'who can stop George doing what she wants to!'

George is a fearless, determined member of the Five who always plays an important and active part in their exploits. She is held prisoner by villains and kidnapped several times, yet the only time she ever shows any sign of fear is when Timmy is in danger. But crooks and villains had better watch out if they make her angry or threaten Timmy, for sparks are sure to fly before the end of the adventure!

WHERE IS KIRRIN ISLAND?

. . . and other locations in the Famous Five books

You won't find Kirrin or Kirrin Island on any map of Great Britain but Enid Blyton did base these and some other places mentioned in the Famous Five books on actual places that she had seen, visited or heard about.

KIRRIN CASTLE

Our first clue as to where we might find Kirrin Castle comes in Enid Blyton's *Children's Page* letters, published in *Teachers World* on 20 May 1931, where she writes about a castle she had visited.

'As I drove along in my little car I saw, far away in the distance, a rounded hill, and on it was the ruin of an old, old castle.'

She goes on to tell her readers that at first she thought the castle looked lonely until she saw that hundreds of jackdaws nested in the ruins and rabbits, so tame that they popped out of their holes, frisked right up to her, and played in the deserted courtyard. She does not mention the name of the castle but a photograph printed with the letter showed it to be Corfe Castle in Dorset. Could this be the castle that gave Enid the idea for Kirrin Castle?

The answer to this question is possibly yes as we know that Enid loved the county of Dorset and often spent holidays in Swanage, the seaside town about ten miles from Corfe. On her visits to Swanage she would have to pass the imposing ruined tower of Corfe Castle that can be seen from several miles as the castle is approached.

There are several similarities between Corfe and Kirrin. They are both built of white stone and both have only one large tower still standing. Probably the biggest clue to Corfe being Enid's inspiration for Kirrin is the big arched entrance to the inner part of the castle. At Corfe this huge archway has a great break across it and one side has slipped downwards several metres. When the Five first go to Kirrin Castle we are told that they 'gazed at the enormous old archway, now half broken down.' Both Kirrin and Corfe have jackdaws nesting in their towers and although the chances of seeing rabbits running around the courtyard at Corfe are slight these days, when Enid first visited the castle it had few visitors so, her story

about the rabbits is posibly true!

Another possible location for Kirrin Castle was suggested in a letter Enid wrote in 1962 wherein she mentions an island she once visited in Jersey: 'It had an old castle there and I longed to put the island and castle into a book. So I did, as you know!' Corfe or Jersey: the truth is that Kirrin Castle was mainly located in Enid Blyton's wonderful imagination.

KIRRIN ISLAND

If you look on a map of Dorset you will see that Corfe Castle is situated in an area known as The Isle of Purbeck – it is not really an island at all but a peninsula with the sea ten miles away. So where did Enid get the inspiration for Kirrin Island? Some people have suggested Brownsea Island in Poole Harbour but this seems unlikely as Enid did not visit Brownsea until several years after *Five On A Treasure*

Island was published. The real answer to the Kirrin Island question was, however, finally cleared up by Trevor Bolton who corresponded with Enid from 1948 until the early 1960s. In his letters he often asked questions about her books and stories. In one letter he asked if Kirrin was based on a real place and in her reply she said: 'Yes. Kirrin was based on an actual village, bay – & island – but in the Channel Isles, not England.' We learn from Barbara Stoney's biography that Enid visited Jersey during her honeymoon, in 1924, and if we put these two pieces of information together we can see how Enid's imagination took Corfe Castle in Dorset, placed it on an island she had visited in the Channel Islands many years before and gave us the rock-bound Kirrin Island complete with ruined castle, rabbits and jackdaws.

WHISPERING ISLAND

In a 'Special Note From Enid Blyton', at the beginning of *Five Have a Mystery to Solve*, Enid explains that Whispering Island is based upon an actual island in a 'great blue harbour' and that the golf course and Hill Cottage mentioned in the story can both be found overlooking the harbour.

The great harbour is Poole Harbour, one of the largest natural harbours in the world. Whispering Island is based on Brownsea Island, the largest of the five islands in Poole Harbour. Brownsea now belongs to the National Trust and a large part of it is a nature reserve. Many trees cover the island and, as in the story, the wind continually blowing through them does make a whispering noise.

The island has a castle, known as either Brownsea Castle or Branksea Castle, but this was rebuilt during the eighteenth century and is now used as a holiday centre. The castle is not open to the public but ferry boats run to the island from Poole Quay and for a small landing charge it is possible to walk round the nature trail. Although you will not find the old well or any of the mysterious statues described in *Five Have A Mystery to Solve*, you might be lucky enough to see some of the red squirrels that still inhabit the island. Dogs are not allowed on Brownsea – so if the Five visited again poor old Timmy would have to stay at home!

The golf-course mentioned in the story is still there. Enid and her husband, Kenneth, bought the golf course in Studland Bay, overlooking Poole Harbour in 1951 and usually spent several holidays a year in the area.

FINNISTON FARM

In another 'Special Note From Enid Blyton', this time at the start of *Five On Finniston Farm*, Enid tells her readers that Finniston Farm is 'a real farm in Dorset' owned by her family. She goes on to say that the old chapel is still there and the great Norman door, described in the story, is also still to be found at the entrance to the kitchen. This 'real farm' was, in fact, Manor Farm at Stournton Caundle, near Sturminster Newton in Dorset which Enid and her husband bought in 1956. Enid never lived at Manor Farm but as she loved Dorset and was frequently on golfing holidays in the area, she had plenty of opportunity to visit and help plan how it was to be run. Enid mentioned her farm and the animals on it several times in *Enid Blyton's Magazine*. Enid and Kenneth sold Manor Farm to the present owners in 1962. It is not open to the public.

CASTAWAY

The town of Castaway, in *Five Go To Smuggler's Top* is built on top of a hill surrounded by an ancient wall with one road into the town still running through the original gateway arch. This is very like the beautiful East Sussex town of Rye, which, like Castaway, still has cobbled streets and many shops with diamond-paned windows. Another similarity is that Castaway is surrounded by treacherous marshes, as Rye once was centuries ago, and the land around the rocky hill on which Rye is built is still very low lying and liable to flood. Rye, like Castaway, also has a traditional history of smuggling and in past ages characters like Mr Barling would have been very much at home in Rye, carrying on a brisk trade in smuggled goods! Unlike Castaway the hill upon which Rye is built is not honeycombed with secret passages.

FIVE GO OFF TO CAMP

In these frames adapted from *Five Go Off to Camp*, the speech and captions have dropped out. Can you match the speech in the coloured boxes (1, 2, 3 and 4) with the illustrated scenes (A, B, C and D)?

A

MINUTES LATER...

1

Speaker 1: You were warned! Now you'll be left here till we've finished our business – maybe three days. Maybe three weeks!
Speaker 2: There will be search parties out for us. They will be sure to find us!
Speaker 1: *Nobody* will find you here. Peters – tie 'em up. We're not taking any chances.
Speaker 2: What about Mum? She'll be worried.
Speaker 1: Let her be. It's your own fault.

B

THEY ALL SAT DOWN TO A HUGE DINNER WITH JOCK, AT 'OLLY'S FARM'...

AT LAST...

2

Speaker 1: That's the best bit of living on a farm – you do get plenty to eat.
Speaker 2: I've never had such a lovely dinner in my life, Mrs Andrews.
Speaker 1: I wish I could eat some more, but I can't. It was super!
Speaker 3: Smashing!

C

3
Speaker 1: George! See the stars shining?
Speaker 2: This is super. I never felt so cosy in my life.
George was too tired to care about the stars ...
Speaker 1: Our first night of camping. I shall lie awake and look out at the stars and breathe in the smell of heather.
But she didn't. In half a second, Anne was sound asleep too.

D

4
Speaker 1: The spook train! It's coming back!
Speaker 2: Stand still and watch. It'll be going into the tunnel.
Again, the noise grew thunderous until ...
Speaker 3: So there is a spook train. It came and went – where from or where to, nobody knows.
Speaker 2: But *we've* seen it in the darkness of the night. And jolly creepy it was too!

Answers:
A goes with ___; B goes with ___; C goes with ___; D goes with ___;
If you want to act out the whole scene, you could adapt the complete chapters from the book.
See the answers page to find out where each scene belongs.

RESCUE THE FAMOUS FIVE

Help the Famous Five off the shipwreck and out of the sea and onto Kirrin Island! A game for two or more players.

Julian

Dick

Anne

George

Timmy

You'll need: One dice and one shaker

HOW TO PLAY:

1. Redraw, or copy and cut out the playing cards and counters and stick them on to thin card.
2. Put the cards in the inside part of the game circle, where the name of each character is printed (i.e. all the 'Anne' cards on Anne's name).
3. The player who throws the highest number chooses a counter and goes first.
   Using your counter, move round the outer circle the same number of places as shown on the dice.
4. When you land on a picture of one of the Famous Five, pick up the matching playing card from the centre of the board.
5. The winner is the first to collect a full set of characters.

PLAYING CARDS

COUNTERS

THE FIENDISH FAMOUS FIVE QUIZ ... Part 1

Call yourself a Famous Five expert? Take our quiz to find out for sure. Sometimes, we'll steer you in the direction of a particular book. A full list of Famous Five titles is at the start of this Annual.

1. How many full-length books about the Famous Five did Enid Blyton write?

2. What sort of work does Uncle Quentin do?

3. How did Red Tower get his name? (See book 9)

4. Who were the two crooks looking for stolen jewels at Two Trees? (See book 10)

5. Who goes camping with the Five in *Five Go Off to Camp*?

6. What is the name of the kidnapped scientist in *Five Have a Wonderful Time*?

7. Who owns Old Towers? (See book 17)

8. What are ingots? (See book 1)

9. Julian reads the Latin words *via occulta* on an old piece of linen in *Five Go Adventuring Again*. What does he think the words mean?

10. Where does the secret passage that runs under the sea from Kirrin Island go to?

See page 62 for more questions – and page 64 for the answers!

FIVE GO TO DEMON'S ROCKS

This comic strip is adapted from the nineteenth title in the series.
Don't forget to read Enid Blyton's original book
for the whole story!

IT'S FROM TINKER. IT SAYS WE CAN WALK ACROSS THE SANDS TO THE LIGHTHOUSE AT LOW TIDE, BUT TO USE THE BOAT IF THE TIDE'S IN WHEN WE ARRIVE.

STEADY AS YOU GO, DICK, OR WE COULD RUN INTO THOSE SNAGGLY ROCKS!

WOW! THE SEA IS A LOT MORE CHOPPY THAN IT LOOKED FROM THE SHORE.

ULP! TH-THAT WAS A CLOSE THING, JULIAN!

HO-HO! DO YOU STILL THINK THE SEA IS ROMANTIC, ANNE?

MAKE SURE THE BOAT IS SECURED, JULIAN.

DON'T WORRY, I KNOW WHAT I'M DOING.

THAT MAKES A CHANGE!

HELLO, YOU LOT.

TINKER! IT'S GOOD TO SEE YOU!

GOODNESS, HOW YOU'VE CHANGED! YOU HAD LONG CURLY RINGLETS WHEN I LAST SAW YOU.

THAT MUST HAVE BEEN A LONG TIME AGO!

NOW I WEAR MY HAIR SHORT AND PREFER TO BE CALLED GEORGE.

NO OFFENCE, ER ...OLD CHAP.

COME IN AND MAKE YOUR-SELVES AT HOME.

THANK YOU.

CHITTER-CHITTER!

WHAT ON..?

CHITTER-CHATTER!

EEEEEK!

WH-WHAT IS IT?..G-GET IT OFF!

HEE-HEE!

DON'T PANIC! IT'S ONLY MY PET MONKEY, MISCHIEF!

I HOPE YOU DIDN'T THINK I WAS SCARED. I...ER...KNEW IT WAS A MONKEY ALL THE TIME.

DON'T TELL FIBS, DICK. WE KNOW YOU WERE PETRIFIED.

NO, I WASN'T!

YES, YOU WERE!

FOR GOODNESS' SAKE, STOP ARGUING.

YES, IT'S TIME TO HAVE A SNACK.

THIS IS A SNACK?

LATER WE'LL GO DOWN TO THE SHIPS CHANDLER IN THE VILLAGE TO STOCK UP FOR THE NEXT WEEK.

WE CAN HAVE A PROPER MEAL LATER TONIGHT.

I DON'T THINK I COULD FACE ANOTHER MEAL FOR A WEEK!

WE HAVE EASY ACCESS TO THE VILLAGE AT LOW TIDE.

HMMM... BUT WE'LL HAVE TO BE CAREFUL NOT TO GET STRANDED ON THE OTHER SIDE WITHOUT THE BOAT.

MEANWHILE, AT THE SHIPS' CHANDLERS...

I'D LIKE TO BUY A POWERFUL TORCH, PLEASE.

CERTAINLY, SIR, WE'VE THE VERY THING.

HOW ABOUT THIS?

YES, THIS WILL DO FINE... ER...COULD YOU TELL ME WHERE TO FIND DEMON'S ROCK?

IT'S JUST SOUTH OF THE VILLAGE, SIR. RIGHT AFTER A GREAT BIG LIGHTHOUSE. YOU CAN'T MISS IT.

THANK YOU, SIR. WILL THERE BE ANYTHING ELSE?

ER...NOT RIGHT NOW. BUT I'D BE GLAD IF YOU WOULD ANSWER A FEW MORE QUESTIONS FOR ME LATER.

GOOD MORNING, TINKER.

HELLO, WE HAVE JUST WALKED OVER FROM THE LIGHTHOUSE TO BUY ENOUGH TO KEEP FOUR KIDS, ME, A MONKEY AND A DOG WELL FED FOR A WHOLE WEEK!

IT SOUNDS AS IF YOU'LL NEED HALF MY STOCK!

I WOULDN'T BE AT ALL SURPRISED.

TAKE A LOOK AROUND, IT'S A WELL STOCKED SHOP.

OKAY, TINKER.

JUST TAKE CARE NOT TO WAKE OL' CAP'N BOOGLE UP, WILL YOU? HE'S HAVING A QUIET NAP AROUND THE BACK OF THE VEGETABLE RACK.

OH!

HE MUST BE CAPTAIN BOOGLE

SNO-O-O-RE

OH DEAR!

ULP! MISCHIEF IS GOING TO WAKE HIM UP!

CHITTER-CHITTER!

CHITTER!

WHAT'S HAPPENIN'? WHASSERMARRER? GET ORFF ME 'EAD!

I'M SORRY, SIR, WE DIDN'T MEAN ANY HARM.

LOR' LUV YER, M'DEAR... THAT DON'T WORRY ME ONE BIT. THERE'S BEEN TIMES WHEN I'VE 'AD BARBARY APES A'JUMPIN' ALL **OVER** ME!

OOOOH! THAT MUST HAVE BEEN **TERRIBLE!**

NOT NEARLY AS TERRIBLE AS SOME THINGS THAT 'APPENED AROUND 'ERE, M'DEAR!

WHAT'S THE CAPTAIN UP TO, NOW?

NOTHING MUCH, MR. BEAL. HE'S FOUND A NEW AUDIENCE FOR HIS OLD STORIES, THAT'S ALL.

BACK IN TH' OLD DAYS THERE WAS SHIP-ROBBERS OPERATIN' OUT OF OUR VILLAGE!

SHIP-ROBBERS! WHAT WERE THEY?

AH, WELL YOU MIGHT ASK, M'DEAR...SHIP-ROBBERS WERE KNOWN AS 'WRECKERS' IN OTHER PARTS OF THE COUNTRY.

27

THEY WOULD RIG UP A DECOY LIGHT ON THE CLIFFS.

WASN'T THAT A BIT DANGEROUS?

'TWERE MORE THAN A BIT DANGEROUS, T'WERE DOWNRIGHT **DEADLY**! SHIPS ENDED UP ON DEMON'S ROCKS WHERE THE SHIP-ROBBERS COULD PLUNDER THEM AND MURDER THEIR CREWS!

WHAT A VERY NASTY THING TO DO!

H-HOW LONG AGO D-DID ALL THIS HAPPEN?

NOT SO MANY YEARS AGO. IN FACT 'TWERE MY GRANDFATHER, JOSHUA, WHO BROUGHT 'EM TO JUSTICE!

CAN YOU TELL US ALL ABOUT IT, CAPTAIN?

HA-HA! I'D LIKE TO SEE ANYONE **STOP** THE CAP'N TELLING HIS STORY!

NEVER MIND. MY YOUNG FRIENDS ARE SURE TO ENJOY IT.

YOUNG JOSHUA WOULD' HA' BEEN ABOUT TWELVE YEARS OLD WHEN HE WAS MAKING HIS WAY HOME ALONG THE CLIFF TOP, ONE DARK AND STORMY NIGHT...

THEN, LOOKING OVER THE SIDE OF THE CLIFF HE SAW 'ONE-EAR' BILL LOOMER AND HIS TWO SONS RIGGIN' UP A DECOY LIGHT...

HE WAS A WITNESS TO WHAT 'APPENED WHEN THAT DECOY LIGHT LURED A PASSING SAILING VESSEL ON TO THE DEMON'S ROCKS...!

OL' ONE-EAR AND HIS HENCHMEN OVERRAN THE SHIP AND KILLED ITS CREW!

BUT ONE-EAR SPOTTED POOR LI'L JOSHUA, AN' HE DETERMINED THAT THE LAD SHOULDN'T LIVE TO BEAR WITNESS AGAINST HIM AN' HIS SONS.

JOSHUA TRIED TO RUN AWAY, BUT THE LOOMERS GAVE CHASE.

THE LAD WAS SCARED OUT OF HIS WITS, THE LOOMERS WERE INTENT ON CATCHING HIM BEFORE HE COULD GIVE THEM AWAY.

COME BACK, YE YOUNG SWAB!

MY OL' GRANDAD'S LUCK WAS OUT, AN' HE TRIPPED ON A BIT OF DRIFT-WOOD.

HE WAS AT THE MERCY OF THE SHIP-ROBBERS!

HAR-HAR! WE'VE GOT 'IM NOW!

SLIT 'IS GULLET OPEN!

BUT HIS MOTHER HAD RAISED THE ALARM WHEN JOSHUA HAD FAILED TO COME HOME, AND THE LOCAL EXCISE MAN HAD LED THE SEARCH THAT DISCOVERED THE LOOMERS.

STOP! I HAVE YOU COVERED WITH MY PISTOL!

WE'RE CAUGHT!

MORE FUN AND GAMES

The Famous Five isn't just about books. Have a look at these games and recordings from over the years.

FREE SWAP CARD *Inside*

The Australian
CHUCKLERS WEEKLY

BRAND **NEW**
Enid Blyton
STORY
FIVE GET INTO
A FIX
see page 10

Australian comic, 1958

A board game from 1978

Enid Blyton's
FAMOUS FIVE

KIRRIN ISLAND
Treasure
Quest

A fabulous adventure game for 2 to 4 players.
Setting sail from Kirrin Island in your own boat to find each of 5 different treasures.

Based on the popular television series.

1993

THE FAMOUS FIVE
Enid Blyton
FIVE ON A
SECRET TRAIL

READ BY JAN FRANC

This stationery set dates from the mid-1950s

Enid Blyton's
"FAMOUS FIVE"
Stationery

THE FAMOUS FIVE CLUB

BEST WISHES

A birthday card produced in 1955

Enid Blyton's
FAMOUS FIV
Five Go to Mystery Moor
Annu

The 1980 Famous Five Annual

A recording from 1975

1983

A recording from South Africa from 1982

A Pepys Game, 1978

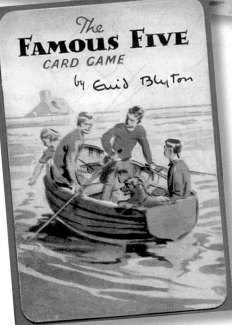

This card game dates from 1951

1975 jigsaw puzzle

FAMOUS FIVE FIND-A-WORD

Can you find the words hidden in the puzzle? They might be forwards, backwards or on a diagonal.

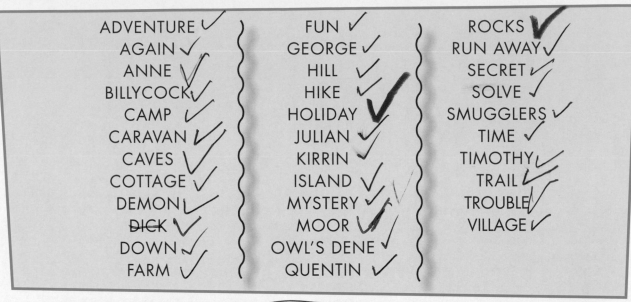

ADVENTURE ✓
AGAIN ✓
ANNE ✓
BILLYCOCK ✓
CAMP ✓
CARAVAN ✓
CAVES ✓
COTTAGE ✓
DEMON ✓
DICK ✓
DOWN ✓
FARM ✓

FUN ✓
GEORGE ✓
HILL ✓
HIKE ✓
HOLIDAY ✓
JULIAN ✓
KIRRIN ✓
ISLAND ✓
MYSTERY ✓
MOOR ✓
OWL'S DENE ✓
QUENTIN ✓

ROCKS ✓
RUN AWAY ✓
SECRET ✓
SOLVE ✓
SMUGGLERS ✓
TIME ✓
TIMOTHY ✓
TRAIL ✓
TROUBLE ✓
VILLAGE ✓

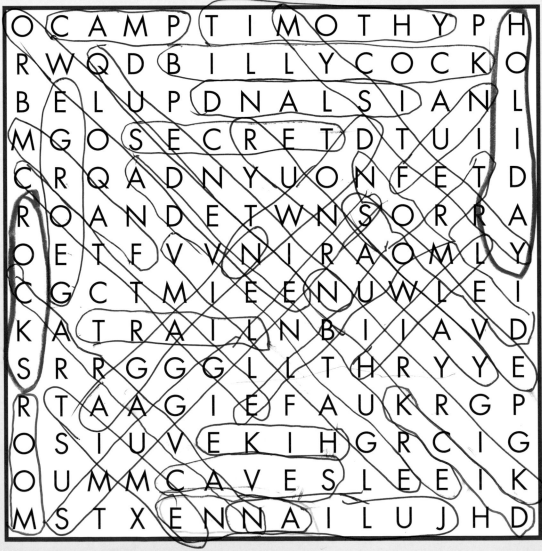

THE FIVE'S FRIENDS

While adventuring the Five encounter many friendly and helpful people.

Note: The number at the beginning of each entry refers to the number of the Famous Five book in which the character appears.

Richard fleeing from Mr Perton in *Five Get into Trouble*.

Aggie (8): When the Five are prisoners at Owl's Dene they find a friend in Aggie, the down-trodden housekeeper of Mr Perton. Aggie has a miserable life, made worse by the bad-temper of her brother, Hunchy. The children are friendly towards Aggie and in return she sees that they have plenty of food. She warns them that Hunchy plans to poison Timmy.

Aily (17): The small, wild looking girl who roams the Welsh mountains and, dressed only in ragged shorts and blouse, seems almost oblivious to the cold. Aily, with her 'face as brown as an oak apple,' wanders the mountainside with her lamb, Fany and her dog, Dave, singing in her 'high, sweet voice.' At first she is nervous of the Five but their kindness reassures her and she is soon treating Julian like an elder brother. Aily cannot read but she has a wonderful sense of direction and shows the Five how to get into Old Towers where they believe Bronwen Thomas is being held prisoner.

Jennifer Mary Armstrong (3): Jenny Armstrong is a little girl kidnapped by the Stick family and held prisoner on Kirrin Island. Despite her young age she shows great courage when the Five rescue her from the dungeons of Kirrin Castle and wants to stay with them on the Island when the adventure is over. Like Anne she loves dolls – her own four dolls are named Josephine, Angela, Rosebud and Marigold. Jenny is a small girl with large dark eyes and dark red hair that tumbles over her cheek. She lives close to the sea with her parents. Her father, Harry Armstrong, is a millionaire and a ransom of £100,000 was demanded for her safe return.

The Barnies (12): A group of travelling players who give theatrical performances to villagers in Cornish barns. Their repertoire includes singing, dancing, fiddle playing and the hilarious performance of Clopper, 'the funniest horse in the world.' At each stop they clear a barn, build a stage of planks supported on barrels, set up their home-painted scenery and give a number of evening performances. Their boss is the Guv'nor, who uses the Barnies' theatrical activities as a cover for smuggling.

Ben the blacksmith (13): A big, eighty year old blacksmith with a mane of white hair who has lived close to Mystery Moor all his life. He only appears once in the story but tells the children the story of The Bartles and how Mystery Moor got its name.

Fair Folk (11): While staying near Faynights Castle the Five camp in the same field as a number of fair folk. The fire-eater, Alfredo, is the uncle of their friend Jo. In *Five Have a Wonderful Time* a number of the fair folk help the Five when they are held captive in the tower room at the top of Faynights Castle. These include: Mr Slither the snake man, Bufflo the whip expert and his wife, Skippy, and Jekky the rope man.

Jenny (21): The long-suffering maid of Professor Hayling at Big Hollow House. Jenny is a wonderful cook, with a character similar to that of Joan, the cook at Kirrin Cottage. She has sharp ears and hears the quiet noises made the night Professor Hayling's secret papers are stolen. She feels the cold and does not like swimming.

Mr Gaston (10): A wealthy man who lives at Spiggy House close to Beacons Village on the moor. Mr Gaston owns a number of horses and is something of an amateur vet. When Timmy hurts himself climbing down a rabbit hole, Mr Gaston is able to put it right. Later, when the Five have successfully found a large quantity of stolen jewels, it is Mr Gaston whom they telephone for help. He comes in his car to fetch them and takes them to see the police inspector at Gathercombe where they not only hand over the jewels but are also given the chance to wash and change before going back to their schools.

Grandad (12): Yan's great grandad is over ninety but still lives in a tiny shepherd's hut and works as a shepherd on Tremannon Farm. He isn't very big, seems shrivelled like an over-stored apple and has a face with a thousand wrinkles. His hair and beard are as grey as the sheep he tends. He tells the Five of the Wreckers' Tower where, almost a century before, his father used to shine a false light on stormy nights to lure ships to their destruction. Grandad tells the children that on wild nights the light still shines from the tower. Grandad goes to the show given by the Barnies and thoroughly enjoys it, but tells everyone that he is only there for the slap-up supper that follows the performance!

Professor Hayling (19/21): The scientist father of Tinker Hayling who is even more forgetful than Uncle Quentin! He forgets his meals, leaves papers in the wrong place and never remembers when he has asked people round to visit. He keeps his most important papers in a tower built in his garden. The professor smokes a pipe and has a tremendous laugh.

Tinker Hayling (19/21): The nine year old son of Professor Hayling who comes to stay at Kirrin Cottage with his pet monkey, Mischief, while his father and Quentin Kirrin discuss important work. Tinker is obsessed with cars and spends most of his time running around imitating the noise of a car or lorry engine. When the noise of all the children and the two animals eventually becomes too much for the two scientists, Tinker hits upon the idea of taking the Five to stay in the lighthouse he owns at Demon's Rocks.

The Five next meet Tinker when they go to stay with him at his home, Big Hollow House, a bus ride away from Kirrin. On this second visit he is not quite so obsessed with cars!

Henry (Henrietta) (13): A tomboy of about the same age and build as George. Henry is wiry and strong, has a broad grin and is an excellent rider. She likes to stride about in her riding jodhpurs whistling. She has three brothers, and two great-aunts who fuss over her. George is jealous of Henry and is annoyed when Julian and Dick mistake her for a real boy! The two girls gradually become friends and when Anne and George are held captive on Mystery Moor Henry plays a big part in their rescue.

Bobby Loman (22): An orphan aged about eleven who lives in Kirrin Village with his Grandfather. Bobby has two pets: Chippy, a mischievous little monkey, and Chummy, a cross-breed Alsatian dog. When Chummy bites someone and his grandfather threatens to have the dog destroyed, Bobby runs away to Kirrin Island. The Five find him there and persuade him to return to Kirrin Cottage with them. The problem is eventually resolved when grandfather says he will have the dog properly trained.

Henry and Harriet Philpot – 'The Harries' (18): Despite one being a girl and the other a boy Henry and Harriet look identical.

Once the twins have made friends with the Five they let them into the secret that Harry has a scar on his hand where he once cut it on barbed wire.

Jonathan Philpot (18): Known by all as Great Grand-Dad, old Jonathan, now getting on for ninety years of age, still does a full day's work around Finniston Farm. He has 'a shock of snowy white hair, a luxurious white beard reaching almost to his waist and very bright eyes.' When not working on the Farm he usually sits in his big chair in the dining room. He has a loud voice which he uses to great effect if he dislikes something he sees. His great friend is William Finniston, owner of a small antique shop in Finniston village, who is a descendent of the original builder of the castle that once stood on a site close to Finniston Farm.

Richard Kent (8): The Five first encounter Richard when they are camping close to the Green Pool, a small lake owned by Richard's millionaire father. He is a well built twelve year old with fair hair, blue eyes and a rather boastful manner. Richard is keen to go part of the way with the Five on their cycling tour and later lies to them that he has permission from his mother to cycle with them as far as Great Giddings, where his aunt lives. Richard is rather a spoilt child. He has a cowardly nature and seems to think only of his own safety. He is easily scared and bursts into tears when the slightest danger threatens. Julian at first thinks that he is 'too feeble for words.' As the story progresses, however, Richard begins to see some of his faults and by the end of the adventure he has changed for the better, thanks to the good influence of the Five.

Guy and Harry Lawdler (15): The twin sons of archaeologist and explorer Sir John Lawdler, both boys take after their father and enjoy excavating Roman remains. When the Five first meet the boys on Kirrin Common they do not realise that there are two of them and continually talk at cross purposes before they realise that they are dealing with twins! Guy, who owns Jet, the little mongrel dog, enjoys joking and tricking while Harry prefers to read a book.

Guy Lawdler

Nobby (5): We never learn Nobby's surname but we do know that he is an orphan and that his father was a clown at Mr Gorgio's circus. He is about fourteen years old, has a freckled face and his favourite expression is 'Jumping Jiminy'. He first meets the Five as the circus procession passes Julian, Dick and Anne's home and after chatting with him the children decide to go on a caravanning holiday to the Merran Hills where the circus is camping. Nobby has a great way with animals and hopes that one day he can work with horses. His best friends at the circus are his two dogs, Barker and Growler, and Pongo the chimpanzee. Nobby has never been to school and can only read a little. He gets on well with the Five and enjoys sharing their picnics and their adventure. He is delighted when Farmer Mackie gives him a job working with the farm horses.

Jock Robins (7): A good tempered boy of about twelve years of age who lives with his mother and step-father at Olly's Farm on the high moors. He has straw coloured hair, blue eyes and a rather red face. Before the death of his real father he lived on Owl's Farm. Jock has never had an adventure before and is very excited at sharing one with the Five.

'Wooden Leg' Sam (7): The grey-whiskered watchman who looks after Olly's Yard. Has difficulty seeing what is going on since he 'bruck his glasses'. He tells the Five of the Spook Train and tells them to keep away from the yard and the railway.

Constable Sharp (19): The hefty policeman at Demon's Rocks who helps the Five to recover some of their stolen property and also assists with the rescue when they are imprisoned in Demon's Rocks Lighthouse. Unlike some of the policemen the Five encounter, P.C. Sharp is very helpful and seems to know what goes on in his village.

Sid (9): The newspaper delivery boy who calls at Kirrin Cottage and who spends the evening with the children while Dick takes his place in order to keep a look out for villains!

Sniffer (13): A thin, wiry little fellow who leads a miserable life with his father, aunt and grandma. His life is made bearable by his love for his dog, Liz and the caravan horse, Clip. Sniffer has a habit of continually sniffing and even when George gives him a large white and red striped handkerchief he prefers to keep it clean and neatly folded rather than use it to blow his nose! Sniffer has plenty of courage and stands up to his father several times in an effort to help the Five. His dream is to live in a house and own a bicycle. After he helps George and Anne escape from captivity George promises that she will buy him a bike.

Spiky (14): A 'short plump boy with a pleasant lop-sided face… eyes as black as currants… and a mop of black hair which sticks up into curious spikes.' He works at Gringo's fair

Sniffer

and gives the children a lead after George is kidnapped.

Mr Tapper (21): (Old Grandad) Owner of the circus that has the right to camp at 'Cromwell's Corner' field once every ten years. 'Old Grandad' is rather fierce looking with a long, bushy beard, enormous eye-brows and only one ear. He has a deep voice but is really a very friendly character. His family have been travelling players since Norman times. Like Jeremiah Boogle, Mr Tapper is liked by all monkeys.

Jeremy Tapper (21): The ten year old grandson of Mr Tapper. Like all of the Tappers he will never give in when arguing and this leads to him having a fight with Tinker. Later the two boys shake hands and become friends.

Derek Terry-Kane (11): A scientist, known to Uncle Quentin, who disappears and is discovered by the Five in Faynights Castle where he is being held prisoner by Jeffrey Pottersham. He has 'big thick arched eyebrows, and (an) enormous forehead.'

Benny Thomas (16): Younger brother of Toby and keeper of strange pets, the latest of which is a pigling named Curly. Benny has yellow curly hair, fat little legs, brown eyes and a high voice. His favourite phrase, when speaking of Curly, is that 'he runned off.' Benny uses this as an excuse for wandering away from the farmyard. Benny's previous pets included a lamb and two goslings.

Jeffrey Thomas (16): Jeff is a Flight Lieutenant at the Billycock Hill Air Force base where he flies one of the experimental fighters. He is a tall, strong, good-looking young man with 'eyes as keen as hawks.' When two planes go missing from the base he, and his friend and fellow pilot, Ray Wells, are suspected of being traitors.

Toby Thomas (16): Julian and Dick's school-mate who lives on Billycock Farm and arranges the camping equipment and food when the Five go to Billycock Hill. Toby is a bit of a joker who enjoys putting caterpillars down people's necks and drenching his school friends with water-squirting imitation roses. During the school holidays he works hard at jobs around the farm including milking cows, cleaning out sheds, collecting eggs and even whitewashing out-houses. His cousin, Jeffrey Thomas, is his great hero.

Tucky (7): The old porter and former railway guard who has worked on the moorland railway since he was a boy. He tells the children all about the network of tunnels running under the moors and gives them an old large scale map of the railways.

Wilfrid (20): A selfish, mannerless boy of about ten years of age with bright blue eyes and yellow hair who is staying at his grandmother's cottage for a few weeks. When the Five arrive to keep him company he is rude and off-hand towards them, telling them to 'clear off!' Wilfrid has a great way with animals and when he plays on a little wooden flute even the most timid of wild creatures come to him. Rabbits nestle in his arms and magpies sit on his head. George is very annoyed that even Timmy goes to him. Under the good influence of Julian, Anne, Dick and George, Wilfrid's character does begin to change and towards the end of his adventure with them he redeems himself by rowing a boat across to Whispering Island where the Five are marooned.

Berta Wright (14): 'A slim, pretty little girl with large blue eyes and wavy golden hair', Berta is the daughter of Elbur Wright, an American scientist working with Uncle Quentin on an amazing new invention 'that will give us heat, light and power for almost nothing!' Berta has no mother but her father, whom she calls 'Pops', dotes on her and when she is threatened with being kidnapped he leaves her with Quentin and Fanny in the hope of putting the kidnappers off the scent. With a few snips of the scissors and a change of clothes Berta is transformed into Lesley with the aim of further confusing kidnappers looking for a long-haired girl! Later Berta is transformed back into a girl and goes to stay with Jo.

Benny Thomas

FIVE ON A TREASURE ISLAND

THE STORY SO FAR: Discovering an old treasure map, the Famous Five race against a crooked antiques dealer to uncover its secrets. Now, in the dungeons of Kirrin Castle …

'Who's there?' The threatening voice boomed out again. Timmy growled louder and louder. He'd protect George and Julian if he could. Yes! And the ingots, too!

George told Timmy to be quiet. Julian switched off his torch and spoke worriedly, without thinking. 'I do hope Dick and Anne are OK!' Then, a man appeared just as the echoes repeated Julian's last few words!

Then the man saw the ingots and gave a low whistle. 'Look at them, Jake! They'll be dead easy to take away!'

'Well, well, well!' said the man. 'Two children in the dungeons of my castle!' A second man stepped forward. 'Never mind all that,' he snapped. 'Who are Dick and Anne? And where are the ingots?'

'They're mine!' George yelled. 'You think you were clever finding out about them from the map in the box you bought and then offering to buy the castle and island. But everything here belongs to our family! And I'm going home right now.'

'We're taking the gold whether we buy the place or not!' sneered Jake. 'You aren't going anywhere! And call this dog off, or else!' Suddenly, Jake was pointing a gun at Timmy!

The second man stepped forward. 'And you're going to write a note to your friends, then send this mongrel off with it! I'll give you a pencil and paper and tell you what to put!'

George wrote down what she was told:

Dear Dick and Anne. We've found the gold. Come on down at once and see it. Georgina.

The man took the note and fastened it to Timmy's collar. Tim growled all the time but George kept telling him not to bite.

'Now tell the dog to go and find your friends!' Jake demanded, waving his gun warningly.

'Find Dick and Anne, Tim!' said George. 'Give them the note!' Tim didn't want to leave George, but he knew from her voice that he had to obey her. He looked up at her and whined, gave her hand a lick and sped off down the passage.

He put his nose to the ground, followed the scent of Dick's and Anne's footsteps and followed them up the rocky steps and into the open air. He stopped in the old yard, sniffing. And before long he was

bounding away, over to the rocks where Dick and Anne were sitting.

Dick was feeling OK now. Anne had pulled the splinter out of his cheek and it had almost stopped bleeding.

'Hello, Tim!' said Dick. 'What are you doing here? Did you get tired of being underground in the dark?'

'Look, Dick! He's got something twisted into his collar!' said Anne. 'It's a note. I bet it's from the others telling us to hurry up and go back down. Isn't Tim clever, bringing it to us?'

Dick took the note from Tim's collar and read it aloud.

'Wow!' said Anne, her eyes shining. 'They've found the ingots. Come on, let's hurry! I can't wait to see them.' But Dick didn't move. He just sat there on the rocks staring at the note.

'What's the matter?' asked Anne, impatiently.

'Don't you think it funny that George should suddenly sign herself Georgina?' Dick replied slowly. 'You know how she hates that name. It's almost … almost as if she's warning us that something's wrong!'

'Don't be so silly!' said Anne. 'What could be wrong?'

'I don't know. But I'm going to take a

look at the inlet and make sure nobody else has landed on the island,' said Dick. 'You can stay here with Timmy.'

But Anne ran round the coastline with her brother, telling him all the time how silly he was being. However, when they came to the inlet …

'There is somebody else here!' said Dick. 'He's come over in a motor boat. And I bet it's that shifty-looking man who bought the box. The same man Uncle Quentin's selling the island and castle to!'

'And he's got George and Julian and he wants us, too!' gasped Anne. 'Then he'll lock us all up and disappear with the gold!'

'We must think hard!' said Dick. 'What are we going to do?'

Dick grabbed Anne's hand and hurried her off to the little stone room where they'd set up camp.

'We mustn't go down into the dungeons!' he said. 'And it'd be no use us going for help in the boat. We'd never find the way in and out of those awful rocks!'

'And now Timmy's gone!' sighed Anne. 'I felt a bit safer while he was here!'

'We'll be OK,' said Dick. But just then they heard angry voices. 'There's two of them!' whispered Anne.

'Anne!' hissed Dick. 'We'll have to hide down the well! They'll never find us there!'

When they reached the well, Anne climbed in first. It was spooky and scary, and Anne's legs felt like jelly! She could hear the men shouting for them. She was glad when Dick joined her and helped her off the ladder, and onto the stone slab that Tim had sat on when he'd fallen into the well.

Soon Jake and his accomplice came close to the well. Close enough to be

overheard! 'There're two locked up and two wandering around. We'll go back and make plans for getting the gold off the island and we'll take the kids' rowing boat with us so they can't escape!'

'The men have blocked the entrance to the dungeon!' he said. 'George and Julian are prisoners and we can't do a thing to help them!' Anne sat down on a stone. After a while she looked at Dick. She was grinning. Had she got an idea?

After what seemed like ages, Dick heard the motor boat being started up. 'It's safe to get out now!' he told Anne. And when

they'd climbed out they stood in the sun and watched the motor boat streaking towards the mainland.

'They haven't taken our boat after all!' said Dick. 'If only we could rescue Julian and George, we could get help. George could row us back.'

'Why can't we rescue them?' asked Anne. Her brother swung her round and pointed.

Now read on! Find a copy of *Five On a Treasure Island* today!

43

TANGLED TITLES

Each letter of the alphabet is represented by a number in these tangled chapter titles from *Five Go Down to the Sea*. Can you work out which letters correspond to the numbers from 1-26?

HERE'S A BIG CLUE!

If you can find out which number this book is in the Famous Five series, it will help you on your way!

23-26-14-22-16-15 20-25 5-19-16 14-12-7-16

Answer: _____

24-26-4-5-23-10 12-13-26-6-5 14-23-26-1-1-16-3

Answer: _____

12 4-5-3-12-25-18-16 5-12-23-16

Answer: _____

15-26-8-25 20-25 5-19-16 14-26-7-16

Answer: _____

5-19-16 4-16-14-3-16-5 1-12-4-4-12-18-16

Answer: _____

26-6-5 20-25 5-19-16 25-20-18-19-5

Answer: _____

Once you've worked them out, write the letters on the line above the number.

—	—	—	—	—	—	—	—	—	—	—	—	—
1	2	3	4	5	6	7	8	9	10	11	12	13

—	—	—	—	—	—	—	—	—	—	—	—	—
14	15	16	17	18	19	20	21	22	23	24	25	26

MEET DICK

Dick is Julian's younger brother and the liveliest human member of the Five! At the time of *Five On A Treasure Island* Dick is eleven years old, the same age as his cousin, George. At the beginning of the story we learn that a few years earlier he had been something of a cry-baby but by the time of their first adventure he has grown out of that and proves himself to be a very resourceful member of the Five.

It is Dick who realises that when George signs 'Georgina' on the note brought by Timmy from the dungeons on Kirrin Island that it is probably a sign that something is wrong. It was Dick's discovery of the hidden recess behind the sliding panel at Kirrin Farmhouse and the secret door halfway down the well-shaft on Whispering Island that led to two of the Five's greatest adventures.

Dick likes a good joke and can usually see the funny side of a situation. He frequently says things purposely to annoy and niggle George in order to see her famous frown! He is good at conjuring and proud of the fact that he is the champion cherry-stone spitter at his school – though he is beaten by Jo when they have a contest!

Perhaps Dick is best known for his love of food. All the members of the Famous Five enjoy tucking in to a good meal but Dick has a particularly healthy appetite! In their very first adventure we learn that 'he was feeling hungry as usual', and in the same story when the children are listing things they need to take with them on their trip to Kirrin Island it is Dick who immediately says 'things to eat.'

Dick is a friendly, reliable, likeable member of the Five who often adds a touch of humour to the stories yet can be resourceful and as brave as his brother and George when action is needed.

THE FIVE THROUGH THE YEARS

Can you put these covers in date order, starting with the 1940s and ending with today? The adults around you might remember some of them from when they were young!

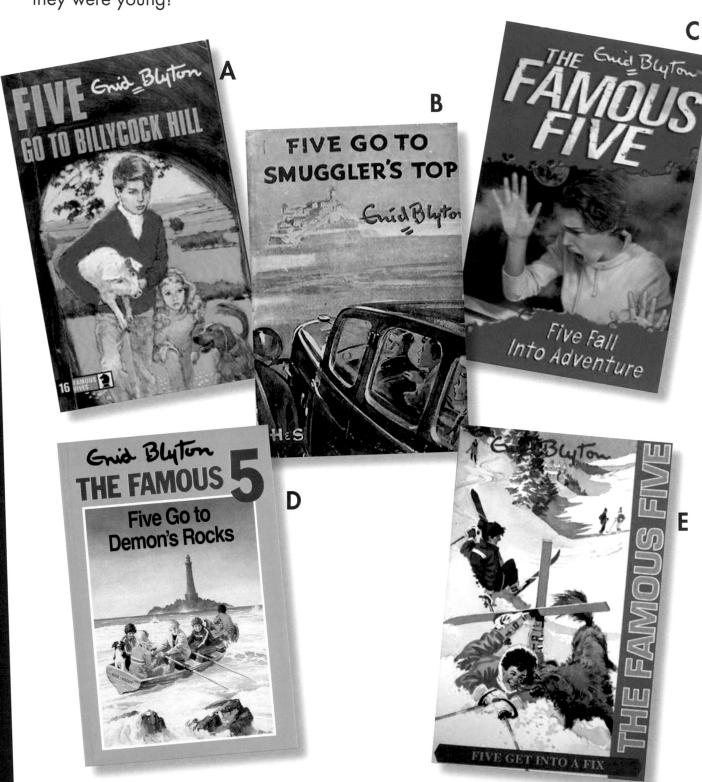

A — FIVE GO TO BILLYCOCK HILL, Enid Blyton

B — FIVE GO TO SMUGGLER'S TOP, Enid Blyton

C — THE FAMOUS FIVE, Enid Blyton, Five Fall Into Adventure

D — Enid Blyton, THE FAMOUS 5, Five Go to Demon's Rocks

E — THE FAMOUS FIVE, Enid Blyton, FIVE GET INTO A FIX

F

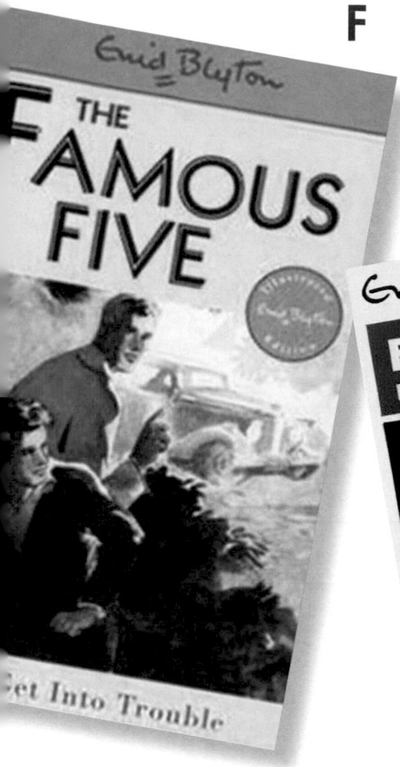

Enid Blyton
THE
FAMOUS
FIVE

Get Into Trouble

G

Enid Blyton   Famous Fives
FIVE
RUN AWAY TOGETHER

a green knight book   3/6

H

Five go to
Smuggler's Top
Enid Blyton

K

Enid Blyton
THE FAMOUS 5

FIVE ON
A TREASURE ISLAND

I

Enid Blyton
FAMOUS FIVE
AS SHOWN ON T.V.

FIVE GO TO
DEMON'S ROCK

J

Enid Blyton
The Famous Five

FIVE ON A TREASURE ISLAND

70TH
ANNIVERSARY
EDITION

COVER BY
Quentin Blake

?

2014 - How would you
illustrate the next generation
of Famous Five covers?

45

MEET ENID BLYTON

Enid's Childhood

Enid Mary Blyton was born on 11 August, 1897 in a small flat over a shop in Lordship Lane, East Dulwich, London. When she was only a few months old the family moved to Beckenham in Kent, an area where Enid and her brothers, Hanly and Carey, spent their childhood.

Enid was fascinated by natural history and was never happier than when she and her father, Thomas, were on long rambles.

Another of her great loves was reading and writing. She read almost everything that she could lay her hands on, even difficult encyclopaedias! Her father encouraged her to write down all the stories and poems she created.

Thomas had been a keen pianist and had always planned for his daughter to have a musical career but in 1916 Enid decided that she really wanted to become a teacher. It was in brief moments of spare time during her teacher training that she first began to write seriously.

Early Poems & Stories

At first Enid could not find a publisher to buy her stories. But she was very determined that she would succeed and carried on writing in every spare moment.

At last she had a short poem published in a magazine run by Arthur Mee and another published in *Nash's Magazine*. We do not know what these first two Enid Blyton poems were because they were both published without an author's name being given. The first poem published under her name was entitled 'Have You . . .?' in March 1917.

She finished her training and started to teach but all the time she still kept on writing. In 1922, she began writing articles for *Teachers World*. From 1929 she wrote a weekly *Children's Page*, which usually consisted of a letter, a poem, and a story. She continued to write regularly for *Teachers World* until 1945.

Of even greater importance was the publication of her first book in the summer of 1922. This was called *Child Whispers* and was a short collection of poems. The book was successful enough for the publisher to issue a further collection, entitled *Real Fairies*, the following year.

Enid Blyton the author was on her way!

On To Success

In 1924 Enid married Hugh Pollock, a publisher. By this time her name was becoming quite well known and larger publishers were beginning to show a great interest in her books.

Two years later, Enid began editing *Sunny Stories for Little Folks*, a fortnightly magazine for younger children. Many of her readers wrote to her and through their letters she gained a good idea of the type of stories they liked to read. Enid made sure that for *Sunny Stories* she wrote the sort of stories that they requested.

Shortly after starting work on *Sunny Stories* Enid wrote a book entitled *The Wonderful Adventure* about a group of six children who searched for a lost treasure. This was Enid's first long adventure story but as the firm that published it was so small few copies were sold. Sadly this early story was soon forgotten and Enid continued to write the short stories that were so popular with readers of *Sunny Stories*. Many of these stories were collected and published as books.

In 1929, when Enid and Hugh moved to Old Thatch, a lovely sixteenth century cottage in Bourne End, Buckinghamshire. This had a much larger garden than Elfin Cottage and gave Enid more space for flowers and pets. It was while at

Old Thatch that her two children, Gillian and Imogen, were born.

For many years Enid filled *Sunny Stories* with short stories, but when the title of the magazine was changed to *Enid Blyton's Sunny Stories*, in 1937, Enid decided to try out a serial story. She called it *Adventures of the Wishing Chair*, and it was so popular with readers that she decided to follow it up with another serial. This time she thought she would try another adventure story and for issue number thirty-seven she wrote the first episode of *The Secret Island*. It was Enid's first full-length adventure story and it was greeted with great enthusiasm.

Soon hundreds of readers were writing in demanding more adventures of Jack, Mike, Peggy and Nora. *The Secret Island* was published in book form in 1938 and a sequel, *The Secret of Spiggy Holes*, started in *Enid Blyton's Sunny Stories* in 1939. Enid knew that children had always enjoyed her short stories but now she saw that her full-length adventure stories were even more popular.

Off on an Adventure

In 1938, Enid and her family moved into a large house in Beaconsfield. In one of her letters for *Teachers World* Enid described the house and its gardens and asked her readers to suggest a name for it. Hundreds of children wrote in, and three-quarters of them suggested the name Green Hedges. Enid lived at Green Hedges for the rest of her life.

The move to Green Hedges saw the start of the busiest period of Enid's life. In addition to writing all of the stories for *Sunny Stories* every fortnight and her weekly page for *Teachers World* she was now also concentrating on full-length books. Best of all her readers loved her adventure and mystery novels. Sadly her marriage to Hugh ended in 1942, just a few months after the publication of the first Famous Five adventure, *Five On A Treasure Island*. In 1943 Enid married her second husband, Kenneth Darrell Waters.

The 'Secret' and 'Famous Five' books were so successful that Enid was soon busy writing other series – including the 'Adventure' series and the 'Mystery' series featuring the 'Five Find-Outers and Dog'.

In March 1949 *The Rockingdown Mystery*, the first book in a series for older children, was published, and later in the year she wrote the first adventure of The Secret Seven. The Seven had first appeared in a book entitled *The Secret of the Old Mill* published a year earlier but The Secret Seven was their first 'official' adventure.

But probably the most important event of 1949 for Enid was the publication of *Noddy Goes to Toyland*. Noddy became Enid Blyton's most popular character for very young children.

Later Days

In the early 1950s Enid stopped writing *Sunny Stories* so that she could concentrate on a new magazine entitled *Enid Blyton's Magazine*. As well as serialising many of her full length books and publishing stories of her other creations, the magazine also ran a number of clubs that helped raise money for good causes. Even the Magazine Club itself helped a charity. The magazine came to an end late in 1959.

During the last few years of her life Enid Blyton suffered from poor health. The death of her second husband, Kenneth, in late 1967, was a great blow to her and she died a year later on 28 November 1968.

Enid, her daughters Imogen and Gillian, and Enid's second husband.

George

Julian

Anne

QUICK ON THE DRAW

Who's the quickest at drawing Timmy – George, Julian, Anne, Dick, Sooty or Marybelle? Play the game and find out!

A game for up to six players. If playing on your own, you could take the part of each character in turn! You will need paper, a pen or pencil, one dice and a shaker.

Dick

Sooty

Marybelle

HOW TO PLAY:
1. Cut out the pictures of the characters and glue them on to separate pieces of thin card. Each player selects which character they want to be and takes it in turn to throw the dice.
2. Using the diagram printed above as a guide, the number you throw determines which bit of Timmy you draw.
3. If you throw a number you cannot use, because you've already drawn that part, then you must skip your go.
4. The first person to draw a complete picture of Timmy is the winner.

RACE TO PACK

A game for up to four players: George, Dick, Anne and Julian. Choose which character you want to be, then trace your character onto thin card and cut it out. This is your counter to move around the squares. You will also need a dice and a shaker.

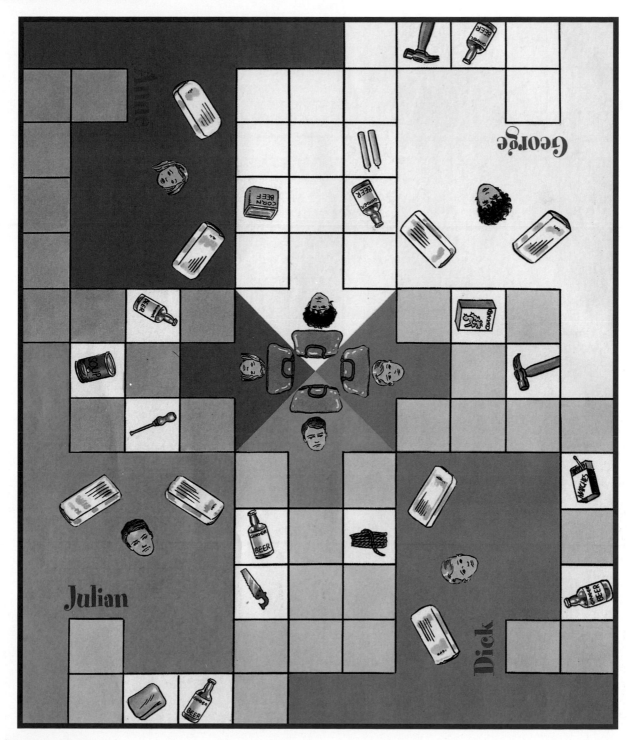

HOW TO PLAY:

1. The player who throws the highest number starts.
2. Move round the board from your starting corner towards your bag in the centre of the board, according to the number shown on the dice. You have to move in a clockwise direction. If you land on a bottle of ginger beer, you can have another go. If you land on any other item, you must miss a turn to stop to pack it into your bag.
3. The winner is the player who reaches their bag first. That means you're all packed, ready for your trip to Kirrin Island.

GOOD OLD TIMMY

'Aren't you ready to come down to the beach and bathe, Anne?' yelled George, standing at the bottom of the stairs. 'We're all waiting for you. Do HURRY UP!'

The study door flew open and Mr. Kirrin, George's father, appeared. 'Georgina! Will you stop shouting all day long? How can I work? For pity's sake, clear out of the house.'

'We're just going, Daddy – and as we're taking a picnic lunch we shan't be disturbing you for some time. I know you're on a big job – it's bad luck it's holiday time and we're here!'

Uncle Quentin grunted and disappeared into his study. Aunt Fanny appeared with two big bags of sandwiches. 'Oh dear – was that your Uncle Quentin shouting again?' she said. 'Never mind! He doesn't mean to be bad-tempered – but he really is on a big job at the moment, and he's trying to get some figures for the scientist he's working with, a Professor

Humes, who is staying in Kirrin – at the Rollins Hotel. Now – here are your sandwiches – and biscuits and apples – and you can take some bottles of ginger-beer out of the larder.'

Just then Anne raced down the stairs, and the Five, all in swim-suits went off to the beach to bathe and laze and play games on the sands. Only three people were there – two men and a lonely-looking boy. Julian found a cool cave and put the food on a shelf of rock.

'What about a swim straight away?' he said. 'Hallo – Timmy's off to rub noses with that dog we saw yesterday – the big ugly brute we didn't much like. He belongs to those two men. They're not much to look at either! I wouldn't like to meet them on a dark night!'

'Well, Timmy seems to like their dog all right,' said George, staring at the two dogs sniffing at one another, then tearing along the sands together, barking happily.

'Look,' said Dick, 'there's that kid coming along the beach again, the one we saw yesterday. Shall we ask him to come bathing with us – he seems to be all on his own. Look out, kid – don't get knocked over by our dog!'

Timmy had come racing up joyfully, chasing the other dog, and the boy went sprawling as they galloped round him. Timmy turned in surprise and saw the boy rolling over and over on the sand. He gave an apologetic bark, and ran to the small boy, licking and sniffing at him.

The boy was terrified of Timmy. He began to scream in terror, and Julian ran to him. 'He's only making friends, he's only saying he's sorry he knocked you over, he won't hurt you! Come on, get up – we were just going to ask you to come and bathe with us.'

'Oh,' said the boy, and stood up, shaking the sand off himself. He looked to be about nine or ten, and small for his age. 'Well – thanks. I'd like to bathe with you. I'm Oliver Humes, and I'm staying at the Rollins Hotel.'

'Then your father must be a friend of our uncle,' said Dick. 'He's called Kirrin – Quentin Kirrin – and he's a scientist. So is your father, isn't he?'

'Yes. A very fine one too,' said Oliver proudly. 'But he's worried this morning.'

'Why? What's up?' said George.

'Well – he's working on something important,' said Oliver, 'and this morning he had a horrible letter. It said that unless Dad agreed to give the writer information he wanted about what Dad was working on, he'd – he'd kidnap me!'

'Oh rubbish!' said Julian. 'Don't you worry about that! We'll tell our dog Timmy to look after you. Just look at him playing with that ugly great mongrel. Timmy's a mongrel too – but we think he's beautiful!'

'I think he's too big,' said Oliver, fearfully, as Timmy came running up, panting. The other dog went back to the two men, who had just whistled for him.

'Come on – let's swim,' said Dick.

'I can't swim,' said Oliver. 'I wish you'd teach me.'

'Right. We will when we've had our bathe,' said Anne. 'We'll go into the water now. Come on!' And soon the Five, Timmy too, were splashing in the sea, yelling and diving in and out, having a glorious time, while Oliver paddled near the shore. Then suddenly Julian gave a shout, and pointed to the beach.

'Look! What's happening there? Hey!' All the Five looked, and saw something very surprising! The two men who owned the big brown dog were dragging Oliver out of the water, one with his hand over the boy's mouth.

'They're kidnapping him! Remember that threatening letter he told us of, that his father had this morning? Come on, quick – see if we can stop them. TIMMY! Come on, now!'

They swam to the shore and slipped hurriedly into their sandals. 'They've taken the kid up the cliffs – they're at the top, look!' panted Julian. 'After them, Timmy!'

But not even Timmy could get up the cliffs in time to rescue the screaming boy. Julian was at the top first, with Timmy – just in time to see a car driving off. The big dog was galloping after it.

'Why didn't they take the dog in the car, too?' wondered Dick.

'Perhaps he's a car-sick dog?' said Anne. 'Anyway, I bet he knows where the men are going, and has been ordered to follow. If the car doesn't go too fast he can easily keep up.'

'I've got the number, anyway,' said Dick.

'Listen – I think Anne's right when she says the dog must know where the men are going,' said Julian. 'And it can't be far away if the dog has to run the whole distance.

Timmy was not listening. He was sniffing the ground here and there. Then he suddenly began to trot along the cliff-road, nose to ground. George gave a sudden exclamation.

'I know! He's sniffing the other dog's tracks – he knows his smell, and he's following it!'

'You're right! Look – let's see if he'll follow the trail properly,' said Julian. 'He might lead

us to Oliver! Tell him, George. He always understands every word you say.'

'Timmy! Listen!' said George, and pointed to some paw-marks made in the sandy road by the big mongrel dog. 'Follow, Timmy, follow. Understand?'

Timmy lifted his big head and looked hard at George, his ears cocked, his head on one side. Yes – he understood. Then, with nose to ground he trotted swiftly away down the cliff-road, sniffing the tracks of the other dog. How did he do it? What a nose he had, old Timmy!

'Come on,' said Dick. 'Timmy will lead us to wherever those fellows are taking Oliver.'

Very steadily, Timmy followed the scent down the cliff-road, turned off to the left, trotted down a lane, swung to the right, then to the left. He waited at the traffic lights, and when they changed to green, he crossed the

road, and then trotted right through the town, nose to trail! The children padded behind in their swim-suits, Anne getting very puffed!

At the other end of the town Timmy turned to the left and padded down a lane, nose still on the scent! The four followed closely. 'I shall have to have a rest soon,' panted Anne.

'I say, that's the car that took the boy away!' exclaimed Dick, suddenly, as they passed a garage, outside which stood a black car, taking in petrol. 'The men are in it. But I can't see Oliver – and that great dog isn't anywhere about, either.'

'Well, they must have hidden Oliver somewhere not far off, and then they came back here for petrol,' said Julian. 'Go on, Tim, old fellow – you're on the right trail. I expect they've left that dog in charge of the boy. I bet if anyone went near, he'd tear them to pieces!'

'And I don't want old Timmy in a dog-fight,' said George.

'Yes. Not so good,' said Julian, and came to a stop. Timmy, however, went on, and wouldn't come back, even though George called him.

'Obstinate old thing!' said George crossly. 'Once he's following a trail nothing on earth will stop him. Well – I'm going after him in case he gets in to trouble!'

'Look – Timmy's gone through that gateway,' said Anne, 'into a field. There's a shed at the bottom of it. Could Oliver be there, with the dog inside, guarding him?'

Timmy stopped suddenly and began to growl. George ran to catch hold of his collar. But Timmy wrenched himself away and raced to the shed, scraping at the wooden door. Immediately a volley of fierce barks came from the shed. The Five halted.

A voice came from the shed. 'Help! Help, I'm locked in here!'

'There – Timmy followed the trail correctly!' said George. 'Quick, Ju – we mustn't let him break in that door – the other dog will fly at him, and at us, too! Whatever can we do?'

It was obvious that the other dog had been left on guard, and would fling himself on anyone or anything that tried to prevent him from doing his duty.

'TIMMY! STOP THROWING YOURSELF AGAINST THAT DOOR!' yelled George. 'YOU'LL BREAK IT DOWN, AND THEN GOODNESS KNOWS WHAT WILL HAPPEN!'

As both dogs, barking fiercely, again flung themselves on it from opposite sides, the door cracked in two places – and the bottom half shook and shivered! 'Anne, George, quick, come with me!' said Julian. 'We may be attacked by that dog once he gets out! Run! We

could perhaps climb that tree, look. Buck up, for goodness sake!'

Terrified, the two girls raced for the tree, and the boys shoved them up, clambering on to a branch themselves.

CRASH! The door fell to the ground, broken in half. At once the great mongrel leapt out. But it took absolutely no notice of Timmy. It ran, instead, to the tree and stood below, growling fiercely. Timmy stood staring in surprise. Why was this dog growling at the children? It was all a mistake, Timmy decided, and he must put it right.

He ran to the tree, and whined as if to say: 'It's all right. Do come down and play with us!' Then he went to the other dog, and whined to him too.

The mongrel gave a loud bark, and jumped up. He ran off a little, stopped and turned round as if saying to Timmy: 'All right – you want a game? Then so do I! You're the dog I played with this morning, aren't you? Well, come on, let's have a game!'

And, to the children's enormous astonishment the two dogs gambolled amiably together!

'I feel a bit silly up here,' said Dick, climbing down. 'Come on – the war's over. Those dogs look as if they're friends for life. Let's go and get that kid.'

With the frightened boy safely in their midst, they began to walk cautiously out of the field. The two dogs took absolutely no notice! The big mongrel had got Timmy down on the ground, and was pretending to worry him. Timmy was having the time of his life!

'Look – there's a bus going to Kirrin!' said Julian, delighted. 'Stop it! We'll get in and take Oliver back to safety while we've a chance. Timmy will just have to walk. He'll make that dog forget all about guarding Oliver!'

It was not very long before they were safely back in Kirrin. Oliver looked very white, but when Julian told him solemnly that it was really a Very Big Adventure, he cheered up and began to boast! 'I was kidnapped! Coo – what will the boys at school say? But I was jolly scared though. Can we go and find my father?'

Professor Humes was very thankful to see his son again, for already he had notified the police that he had disappeared. Dick gave the police the number of the men's car. 'You'll soon track that all right!' he said. 'But not so well as old Tim here – he used his nose, and a jolly good nose it is too!'

'Woof!' said Timmy, and let his tongue hand out of his mouth.

'He says he's hot and thirsty,' said George. 'Let's buy him an ice-cream.'

'We'll ALL have the biggest ice-creams there are in the village-shop,' said the Professor, patting Timmy. 'I could do with one myself.'

'I could do with four,' said Oliver, 'so I hope you're feeling generous, Dad! Dad, you should have seen Timmy following the trail! He's a wonder dog!'

'Well, we've always known that,' said George. 'Come on, Timmy – ICE-CREAMS!'

FIVE HAVE PLENTY OF FUN

Each row contains a word from one of the chapter titles from *Five Have Plenty of Fun*. The number in the blue square tells you which chapter. Can you fill in the correct words? When you have, write down all the letters on the yellow squares. If you unscramble them, you will discover something that happens in Chapter 8!

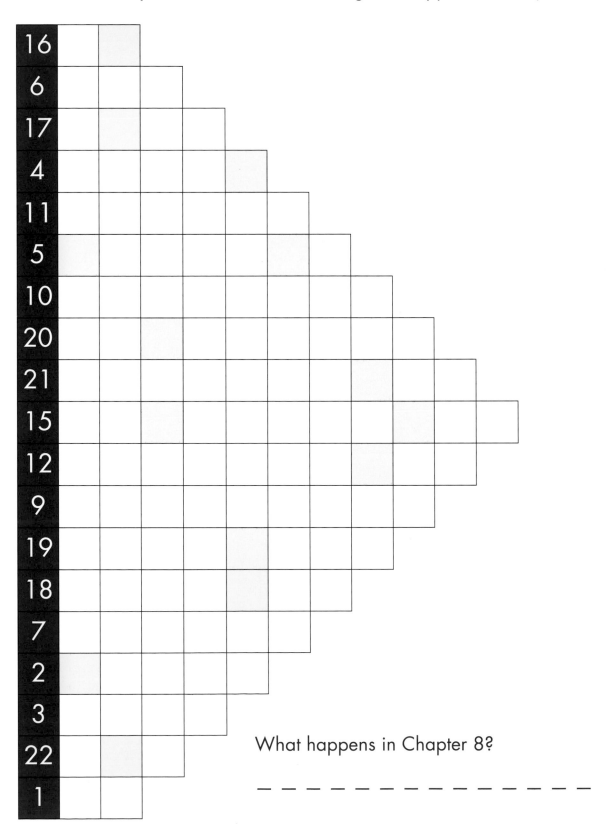

What happens in Chapter 8?

– – – – – – – – – – – – – – – – –

MEET TIMOTHY

Timmy was found as a puppy by George on the moors and taken home to Kirrin Cottage where he disgraced himself by chewing up everything in sight. George's father eventually said that the dog had to go but rather than lose him altogether George gave James/Alf, a local fisherboy, all of her pocket money to look after him for her.

Timmy grew into 'a big brown mongrel dog with an absurdly long tail and a big wide mouth that seemed to grin.' When Julian, Dick and Anne first meet him they find him a 'friendly, laughable, clumsy creature' and all immediately adore him despite the fact that his 'head is too big, his ears too pricked and his tail too long!'

At the end of *Five On A Treasure Island* Timothy is allowed to return to Kirrin Cottage and apart from being banished to an outside kennel for a short time after taking a dislike to Mr Rowland, the tutor in *Five Go Adventuring Again*, he remains with the Five for the rest of their adventures.

Timmy is a big, powerful dog and without him to guard them the Five would not have been allowed to go off on their own.

However, it is not an easy life being a dog with such adventurous owners. He loves plenty of walks and is always happy to go where the children go but his leg joint gets out of place in *Five On A Hike Together* and on several occasions he has to suffer the indignity of being lowered down into caves and pulled up cliffs with ropes tied round his middle. Almost as bad was the time in *Five Go To Smugglers' Top* when he was lowered down into the catacombs in a laundry basket. He is a very clever dog managing to get himself in and out of all sorts of difficult spots but probably his most amazing trick was the way he got himself up the well-shaft in *Five On A Treasure Island* – how he did it we shall probably never know!

When he is not chasing villains or disappearing up secret passages Timmy enjoys sharing the children's activities. He loves standing in the prow of the boat when they row over to Kirrin Island and enjoys swimming with them in Kirrin Bay. He likes sharing their picnics and agrees with the others that Joanna is a wonderful cook. He does not like train journeys, ginger beer or mustard but adores ice cream, a word he knows 'very well indeed.' But best of all Timmy loves his mistress: 'George was the centre of his world, night and day.'

WHAT'S HAPPENING?

Can you match the eight captions from *Five Get into Trouble* below to the eight pictures across these pages?

First, you need to choose from the list of words in the box below. The page numbers refer to the special 'Millennium' Editions of *The Famous Five* which feature coloured versions of Eileen Soper's illustrations.

1. He almost _____ over the excited Timmy, and disappeared thankfully out of the room. (p. 6)
2. The lambs were very inquisitive, and one came right up to Anne and _____ (p. 38)
3. Soon they saw Richard coming, _____ as fast as he could between the trees. (p. 44)
4. Julian moved very cautiously to the shelter of another tree, from where he could _____ better. (p. 71)
5. Hunchy lost his temper suddenly and _____ the shoebrush straight at Julian. (p. 115)
6. Timmy _____terrifyingly, and both Rocky and Mr Perton took some hurried steps backwards. (p. 124)
7. She came out of the kitchen door at that moment, _____ a washing-basket that appeared to be full of clothes. (p. 138)
8. He went to the kitchen window and _____ it wide open. 'RICHARD!' he roared. (p. 152)

   Write the number of the caption that matches the illustration in the box in the top corner of the picture.

Words to choose from:	**Bleated**	**Growled**	**Threw**
	Carrying	**See**	**Swung**
	Fell	**Stumbling**	

MEET ANNE

Anne, the younger sister of Julian and Dick, is ten years old when we first meet her and in the opening chapters of *Five On A Treasure Island* where we learn that she likes dolls, enjoys wearing pretty dresses and finds it difficult to control her tongue. In these ways she is quite different to George, her tomboy cousin, yet the two girls soon become inseparable.

Despite their differences Anne has many of George's qualities. She is loyal and truthful and always prepared to make a personal sacrifice to avoid the others missing out on a treat. Despite not always enjoying adventures while they are actually happening – 'I'm not a very adventurous person, really' – she is brave and resourceful and in many of their adventures displays the greatest brain-power.

Anne is never happier than when the Five are away camping or caravanning and she can organise everything and everybody.

She sees to the cooking, organises the cleaning and bed making and ensures that there is always enough food – not an easy job when dealing with five very large appetites! On these occasions she gives the orders and the other three go 'obediently to work.'

Anne has a quick eye, deft fingers, likes sports and games and is games captain of her form at School. She enjoys horse riding and it is her suggestion that she and George go for a riding holiday at Captain Johnson's riding school while Julian and Dick are away on a school trip (*Five Go To Mystery Moor*). Another of her interests is looking in second-hand shops (*Five On Finniston Farm*). Her favourite colour is red.

Her dislikes include being in very narrow enclosed spaces (such as tunnels and secret passages!), spiders and other creepy-crawlies.

Anne is usually the quietest member of the Five, happy to let one of the others do the talking, but for a time in *Five Have a Mystery to Solve* she turns, as Julian puts it, from a mouse into a tiger. First she throws a bucketful of water over the annoying Wilfrid and later in the same adventure, when two men try to take away the children's boat, she and Timmy chase them off. As Enid writes: 'What chance had any men against a dog and a tiger [Anne]?'

AROUND THE WORLD WITH THE FAMOUS FIVE

Can you match the cover (A-F) with the country from the list below?

1. Finland
2. France
3. Germany
4. Portugal
5. Norway
6. Vietnam

C

B

A

E
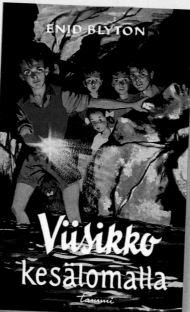

D
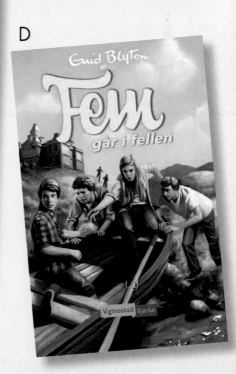

F

THE FIENDISH FAMOUS FIVE QUIZ . . . Part 2

11. Which two places does the secret passage at Finniston Farm run between? (See book 18)

12. Owl's Dene doesn't have a secret passage, but it *does* have a secret room. What is it being used for when the Five visit? (See book 8)

13. How many towers did Kirrin Castle have?

14. What is the name of the disused railway yard looked after by 'Wooden Leg' Sam? (See book 7)

15. In which county of England is *Five Go Down to the Sea* set?

16. Lucas tells the children that Whispering Island has two other names. What are they? (See book 20)

17. What do the villains plan to do to Kirrin Island if Uncle Quentin refuses to give them the results of his secret experiments? (See book 6)

18. Where is Anne hiding when Dick is kidnapped in *Five Get into Trouble*?

19. Where do Julian and Dick hide the forged hundred dollar bills they find on Mystery Moor? (See book 13)

20. What sort of animal is Pongo? (See book 5)

21. Who does Timmy bite when the Five are at Owl's Dene? (See book 8)

22. Sniffer's dog, Liz, can do a number of tricks. Can you name two of them? (See book 13)

23. What sort of a creature is Nosey at Finniston Farm? (See book 18)

24. When they have luggage with them, how do the Five usually travel from Kirrin Station to Kirrin Cottage?

25. What was the name of the boat the Five hired when they stayed at Hill Cottage? (See Book 20)

26. Who owns the circus close to where the Five park their caravan in *Five Go Off in a Caravan*?

27. Who were the family who ran the sand quarry on Mystery Moor, who disappeared suddenly and were never seen again?

28. What surrounds Castaway Hill?

29. What is the name of the castle close to where the Five stay in *Five Have a Wonderful Time*?

30. Where is Dick taken after he is mistaken for Richard Kent and kidnapped? (See book 8)

31. How did the Five open the old box they found in the wreck? (See book 1)

32. Which animals does Timmy love chasing, particularly when he's on Kirrin Island?

33. How do the *Five get to Smuggler's Top*? (See Book 4.)

34. How do the travelling players, known as The Barnies, travel from village to village?

35. What is the name of the tomboy the Five meet at Captain Johnson's Riding School? (See Book 13)

The answers are on page 64.

ANSWERS

FIVE GO OFF TO CAMP

A goes with 3 and is adapted from Chapter 2, 'Up on the Moors'.
B goes with 2 and is adapted from Chapter 7, 'Mr Andrews Comes Home'.
C goes with 4 and is adapted from Chapter 10, 'Hunt for a Spook Train'.
D goes with 1 and is adapted from Chapter 17, 'An Amazing Find'.

FIND-A-WORD SOLUTION

TANGLED TITLES

This is the code: P-1; Q-2; R-3; S-4; T-5; U-6; V-7; W-8; X-9; Y-10; Z-11; A-12 (the clue is *Five Go Down to the Sea* is Book 12 in the series, so that's where the alphabet starts); B-13; C-14; D-15; E-16; F-17; G-18; H-19; I-20; J-21; K-22; L-23; M-24; N-25; O-26.

LOCKED IN THE CAVE
MOSTLY ABOUT CLOPPER
A STRANGE TALE
DOWN IN THE COVE
A SECRET PASSAGE
OUT IN THE NIGHT

THE FIVE THROUGH THE YEARS

The correct order is:
B – 1951; G – 1967; A – 1970; H – 1974; I – 1978; K – 1985; D – 1986; E – 1995; F – 2000; C – 2001; J – 2012;

FIVE HAVE PLENTY OF FUN

JO
FEW
FAIR
BERTA

KIRRIN
MORNING
PUZZLING
THRILLING
UNEXPECTED
DISCOVERIES
SUSPICIOUS
TELEPHONE
EXCITING
HELPFUL
LITTLE
NIGHT
NEWS
ARE
AT

The letters in the yellow squares spell the word: TRANSFORMATION

WHAT'S HAPPENING?

1. Fell
2. Bleated
3. Stumbling
4. See
5. Threw
6. Growled
7. Carrying
8. Swung

AROUND THE WORLD WITH THE FAMOUS FIVE

1. E
2. B
3. A
4. C
5. D
6. F

FIENDISH FAMOUS FIVE QUIZ

1. 21
2. He is a scientist. He writes books and gives lectures.
3. Because of his bright red hair, beard and eyebrows.
4. Dirty Dick Taggart and Maggie Martin.
5. Mr Luffy, one of the teachers at the boys' school.
6. Derek Terry-Kane.
7. Mrs Bronwen Thomas.
8. Blocks of metal. The ones the Five found were made of solid gold.
9. Secret Way.
10. The old quarry on the Moors behind Kirrin Cottage.
11. The cellars of the castle which once stood there, and the old chapel, now used as a grain store.
12. To hide escaped convicts.
13. Two.
14. Olly's Yard.
15. Cornwall.
16. Wailing Island and Keep-Away Island.
17. They plan to blow up the entire island.
18. She has climbed to the top of a tree to keep a lookout for Julian and George.
19. In the funnel of the ancient steam engine that once carried sand from the quarry.
20. A chimpanzee.
21. Rooky.
22. She can walk on her hind legs and do forward rolls.
23. A tame jackdaw.
24. In a pony trap.
25. It was called *Adventure*.
26. Mr Gorgio.
27. The Bartle Family.
28. Marshes.
29. Faynights Castle.
30. Owl's Dene on Owl's Hill.
31. They threw it out of an upstairs window at Kirrin Cottage onto the ground.
32. Rabbits.
33. They travel in a hired car.
34. In old-fashioned open wagons.
35. Henrietta, who likes to be called Henry.

ACKNOWLEDGEMENTS

Timmy's Timeline © Tony Summerfield, 2012

Meet Julian, Meet Anne, Meet Dick, Meet George and Meet Tim, Where Is Kirrin Island?, The Five's Friends, Meet Enid Blyton and Fiendish Famous Five Quiz © Norman Wright 2000 and adapted from *The Famous Five: Everything You Ever Needed to Know*.

George's Hair is Too Long is adapted from the cartoon strip which first appeared in *Enid Blyton Mystery and Suspense* issue 7. The artwork and text from Five on a Treasure Island first appeared in issue 4. Good Old Timmy first appeared in *The Official Enid Blyton Annual, 1997*.

The cartoon strip based on Five Go to Demon's Rocks first appeared in *Enid Blyton's Adventure Magazine*.

Rescue the Famous Five first appeared in *Enid Blyton Mystery and Suspense* issue 1, and Race to Pack first appeared in issue 2. Draw in Timmy is adapted from an activity which first appeared in issue 8.